Sunny Goes to the Beach

A Children's Book on Sun Safety

By Katherine C. Troutman, FNP

Illustrations by Davinia Palmer

Featuring "Sun Facts" for Parents and Caregivers

Sun Facts sourced from the Skin Cancer Foundation

For more information and recommendations, go to:
http://www.skincancer.org/products/categories

Text Copyright © 2016 by Katherine C. Troutman
Illustrations Copyright © 2016 by Davinia Palmer

ISBN-10: 0-9975302-0-0
ISBN-13: 978-0-9975302-0-9

www.sunnygoesto.com

Printed in China

To my guys,
Will and Liam.
~KCT

To the child within all of us:
pure, reliant and with immeasurable potential.
~DP

FIRST 2016 EDITION

A Special Thanks to

Robert Elliott
Paul and Gina Young

Ian Mattingly
Tom Morgan
Stacey Rainaldi
Patti Jefferson

Luke and Penny

Sun Facts
Solar ultraviolet (UV) rays shine every day. Although they are most powerful on sunny, cloudless days, UV rays penetrate rain or shine.

"Sunny! Have you looked out the window today? Not a cloud in the sky. Great beach weather. Hooray!"

"We will head to the beach once you finish your eggs."

"Yippee!" Sunny says. "Let's bring Isla," she begs.

Mom puts sunscreen on Sunny that smells like grapefruits,

Sun Facts

Sun Protection Factor (SPF) is a measure of a sunscreen's ability to filter out UVB, preventing sunburn. SPF 30 filters 97% of UVB.

and they slip on their rash guards, hats, and swimsuits.

Sun Facts
For a day at the beach, choose a broad spectrum (UVA and UVB) and water-resistant sunscreen with at least SPF 30.

"Why do we put sunscreen on before the car ride?"
Mom says, "It has to kick in before we're outside."

Sun Facts
Apply sunscreen 30 minutes before hitting the sand. Rub in 2 Tbsp of sunscreen (golf ball-sized) to all exposed skin. Don't forget the ears, neck, and tops of hands and feet.

Dad loads up the car, and they get on their way.
They stop and grab Isla a few blocks away.

Isla wears sunblock on just her cheeks and nose and no hat or sunglasses or other sun clothes.

Sun Facts
Clothing is our first and best line of defense against UV. Wear tight weave fabrics in dark or bright colors for optimal protection.

At the beach, Dad sets up the shelter and chairs.
Isla says, "We're not camping. Why's a tent over there?"

"The shelter shields our skin and eyes from the sun."

Sun Facts
Beach sunglasses should block at least 99% of UV and cover as much area around the eyes as possible.

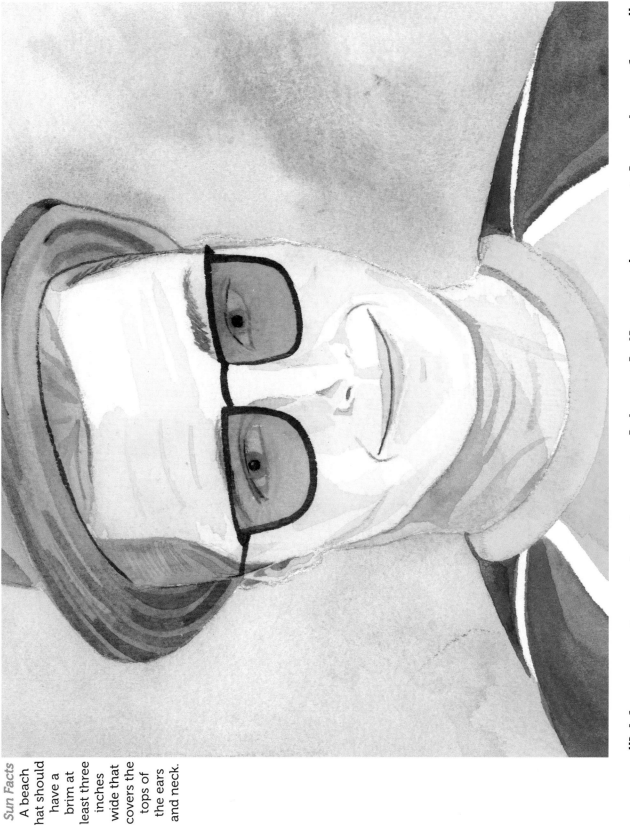

Sun Facts
A beach hat should have a brim at least three inches wide that covers the tops of the ears and neck.

"We must protect our skin while we're out having fun."

Sunny and Isla sink their feet in the sand and race to the water small hand in small hand.

Sun Facts
UV rays are more intense at the beach due to reflection of UV by sand and water. Sand, by an extra 15% and water, up to 10% more.

The girls jump over waves as they splash and they roar.
After an hour, Mom calls them back to the shore.

"Time to put on more sunscreen," Dad says to the pair.
"But we just did that, Dad," Sunny says with a glare.

"When we're swimming, the sun is much more of a threat, and sunscreen won't last for as long when we're wet."

Isla watches a man with a peeling, bald head. "Ouch," Isla whispers, "his skin is beet red."

"Ouch is right! That man should be wearing a hat. His whole day will be ruined with a burn like that!"

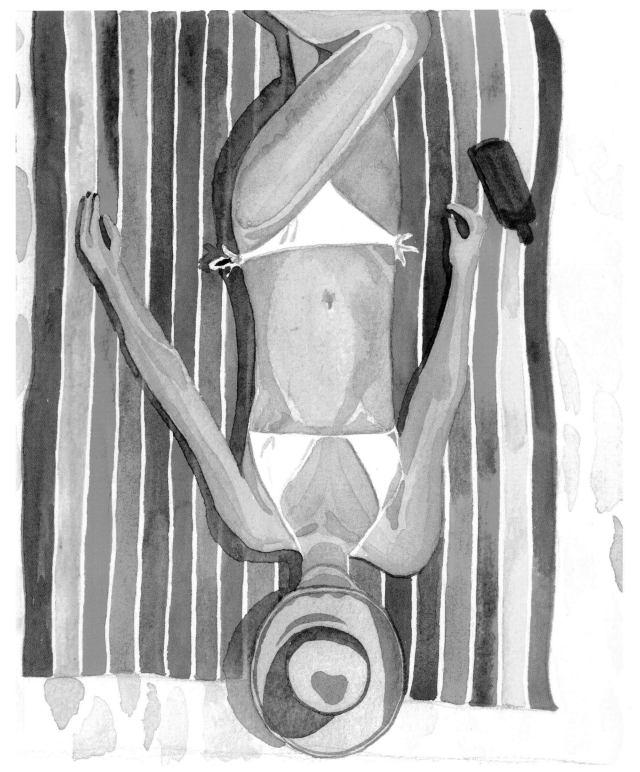

Isla sees a lady lying out getting tan.
"That's more like it since she's not red like that man."

Mom explains, "Even getting a tan hurts our skin.
A tan means too much sun has already snuck in."

Sun Facts
UVA is a long wave ray that causes most of skin aging, while UVB is a short wave ray that causes sunburn.

Mom and Dad sit under the umbrella in shade.

But the girls lie outside of the shadow it made.

Dozing off, Sunny thinks about what she just learned. She moves to the shelter to avoid getting burned.

Sun Facts
Limit direct sun exposure. UV rays are most intense between 10 AM and 4 PM. Seek as much shade as possible during these hours.

Though a cloud hides the sun, Isla's face still feels hot.
She scoots into the tent - it is the best spot.

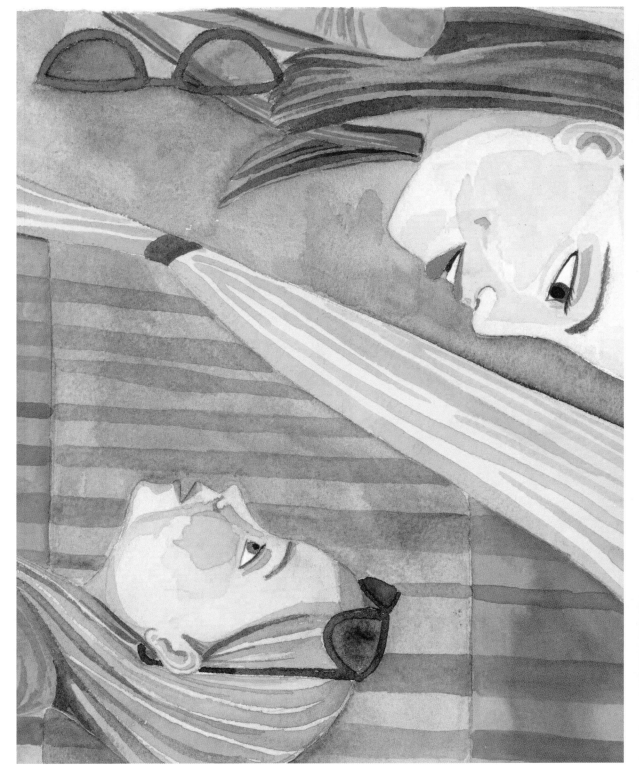

"Safe skin is worth it," Mom says. "Just wait, and you'll see.
Your skin will be healthy when you're older like me."

"I'm getting so sleepy," Dad hears Sunny say.
He can tell they've had enough sun for the day.

The girls help to pack up, so they're off the beach fast. Back at the car, Dad shouts, "Today was a blast!"

On the way back to town, they stop off for a treat.
When your skin is healthy, ice cream tastes extra sweet.